To Jacob.
—G.C.

To Gabi and Kasey.
—M.S.

G. P. PUTNAM'S SONS

A division of Penguin Young Readers Group.

Published by The Penguin Group. Penguin Group (USA) Inc., 375 Hudson Street, New York, NY 10014, U.S.A.

Penguin Group (Canada), 90 Eglinton Avenue East, Suite 700, Toronto, Ontario M4P 2Y3, Canada

(a division of Pearson Penguin Canada Inc.).

Penguin Books Ltd, 80 Strand, London WC2R 0RL, England.

Penguin Ireland, 25 St. Stephen's Green, Dublin 2, Ireland (a division of Penguin Books Ltd.).

Penguin Group (Australia), 250 Camberwell Road, Camberwell, Victoria 3124, Australia (a division of Pearson Australia Group Pty Ltd).

Penguin Books India Pvt Ltd, 11 Community Centre, Panchsheel Park, New Delhi - 110 017, India.

Penguin Group (NZ), 67 Apollo Drive, Rosedale, Auckland 0632, New Zealand (a division of Pearson New Zealand Ltd).

Penguin Books (South Africa) (Pty) Ltd, 24 Sturdee Avenue, Rosebank, Johannesburg 2196, South Africa.

Penguin Books Ltd, Registered Offices: 80 Strand, London WC2R 0RL, England.

Manufactured in China by South China Printing Co. Ltd.

Design by Ryan Thomann. Text set in Archer.

The art was done in watercolor, gouache and mixed media.

Library of Congress Cataloging-in-Publication Data

Choldenko, Gennifer, 1957– A giant crush / Gennifer Choldenko ; illustrated by Melissa Sweet. p. cm.

Summary: Too shy to approach the girl he likes, Jackson hides little gifts for her to discover before Valentine's Day.

[1. Bashfulness—Fiction. 2. Valentine's Day—Fiction. 3. Schools—Fiction.] I. Sweet, Melissa, 1956– ill. II. Title.

PZ7.C446265Gi 2011 [E]—dc22 2009040110

ISBN 978-0-399-24352-3

1 3 5 7 9 10 8 6 4 2

A GIANT CRUSH

story by
Gennifer Choldenko

pictures by
Melissa Sweet

G. P. PUTNAM'S SONS ♥ AN IMPRINT OF PENGUIN GROUP (USA) INC.

$\mathcal{M}$y best friend, Jackson, has been making valentines all day long.

"Who's the special valentine for, Jackson?" I ask.

"It's not special, Cooper," Jackson says.

"Really?" I say. "How come it's so full of chocolate Kisses you can barely close it?"

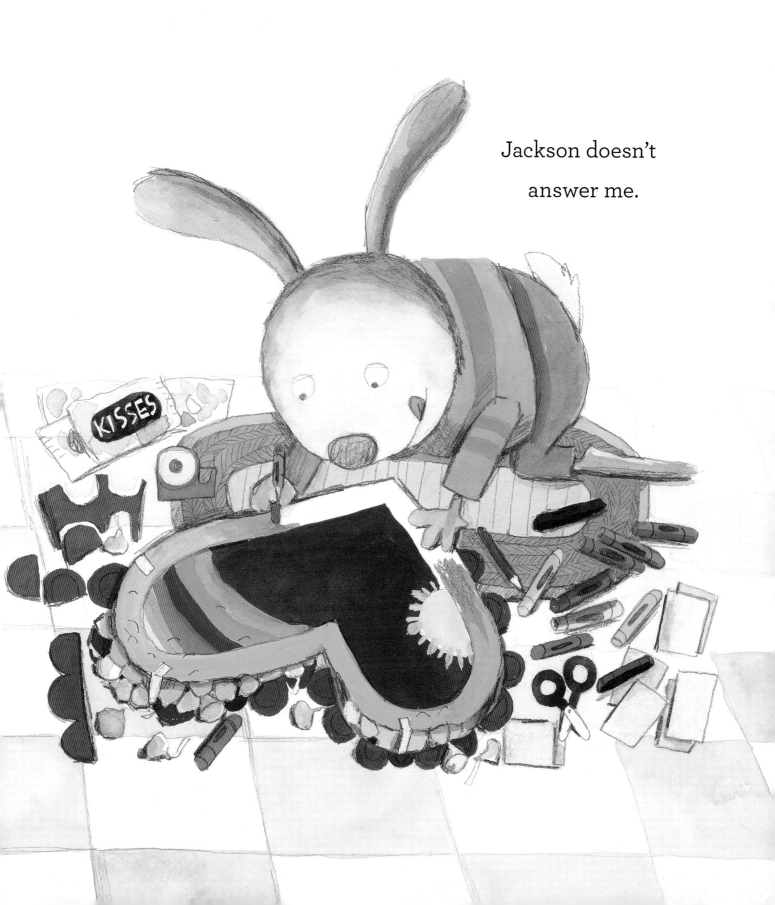

Jackson doesn't
answer me.

On Monday, Jackson comes to school
with a giant yellow flower.

By show-and-tell, the flower's gone.

At recess, Carter Corey
steals the ball from Jackson
and dribbles down to Cami.

He swipes Cami's scarf
and stuffs it in his pocket.

Jackson gets the ball back, but all the girls are chasing
Carter Corey. No one is playing soccer anymore.

"Carter and Cami sitting in a tree, k-i-s-s-i-n-g,"
all the girls sing.

The next day, Jackson has chocolate hearts
in his lunch. I'm hoping he'll give me some,
but when we get to the cafeteria, they're gone.

"What happened to the candy, Jackson?"

Jackson's cheeks flush red as a wrong-answer pencil.

After school, Jackson watches the girls play soccer.
Carter Corey comes over. He climbs the fence and
shouts, "Look at me, I'm even bigger than Jackson. . . .
I'm a giant. Fee-fi-fo-fum!"

All the girls laugh and Jackson turns red again.

On the way home, Jackson drags his backpack bumpity-bump along the pavement.

"What's the matter, Jackson?"

"Carter Corey likes Cami," Jackson whispers.

"Does she know who the flower's from?"

Jackson shakes his head.

"Does she know who the candy's from?"

Jackson puckers his lip out.

"How's she supposed to know you like her?"
Jackson's face crumples up. "I would know
if she liked me," he whispers.

"If you're going to like a girl, Jackson,
you have to at least tell her."

Jackson kicks a can bangity-bang down
the sidewalk. "What if she doesn't like me?"

"Why wouldn't she like you?"

Jackson's eyes are fixed on the ground.
"Because I'm a giant, Cooper."

"Yeah . . . so? Is she too tiny for you?"

"Of course not!

She's perfect . . .

perfect in every way."

Finally, Valentine's Day is here. Right before recess, Miss Moscrop delivers the valentines. She puts Jackson's valentine on Cami's desk.
"Cami has a boyfriend.
Cami has a boyfriend," the girls all chant.

Jackson's head sinks low.

Just then the bell rings. Cami shoves back her chair.
It clatters to the ground. "Does anyone want to play soccer?"
she asks, her face as pink as a valentine heart.

I give Jackson a shove. He takes a wobbly step forward and knocks his chair over too. All the girls giggle.

Jackson and Cami
play two-person soccer
all recess long.

At the end of the day, we race to the cubbies.
When Cami grabs her book, it falls open; pressed
between the pages is the big yellow flower.
"Who gave you that?" Carter Corey wants to know.

Cami's face turns pink all over again.

Carter looks from Cami to Jackson and back again.

"It was Jackson. A giant is your boyfriend?"

"I do not have a boyfriend, Carter Corey," Cami tells him.

"But if I did have a boyfriend, he would be totally giant."

"Cami likes you," I whisper to Jackson.

Jackson throws his backpack in the air.

"Yes she does, Coop. **Yes she does!**"

JAN 2012